MW01053195

Dear Avery,

Happy 4th Birthday!

Love
Nana & Papa

Ladybug Girl

by David Soman
and Jacky Davis

Dial Books for Young Readers
an imprint of Penguin Group (USA) LLC

To our parents, for everything, and
to Lucy and Sam, for more

DIAL BOOKS FOR YOUNG READERS
A division of Penguin Young Readers Group
Published by The Penguin Group
Penguin Group (USA) Inc., 375 Hudson Street, New York, NY 10014, U.S.A.
Penguin Group (Canada), 90 Eglinton Avenue East, Suite 700, Toronto, Ontario, Canada M4P 2Y3
(a division of Pearson Penguin Canada Inc.)
Penguin Books Ltd, 80 Strand, London WC2R 0RL, England
Penguin Ireland, 25 St. Stephen's Green, Dublin 2, Ireland (a division of Penguin Books Ltd)
Penguin Group (Australia), 250 Camberwell Road, Camberwell, Victoria 3124, Australia
(a division of Pearson Australia Group Pty Ltd)
Penguin Books India Pvt Ltd, 11 Community Centre, Panchsheel Park, New Delhi - 110 017, India
Penguin Group (NZ), Cnr Airborne and Rosedale Roads, Albany, Auckland 1310, New Zealand
(a division of Pearson New Zealand Ltd)
Penguin Books (South Africa) (Pty) Ltd, 24 Sturdee Avenue, Rosebank, Johannesburg 2196, South Africa
Penguin Books Ltd, Registered Offices: 80 Strand, London WC2R 0RL, England

Text copyright © 2008 by Jacky Davis
Pictures copyright © 2008 by David Soman
All rights reserved
The publisher does not have any control over and does not assume any
responsibility for author or third-party websites or their content.
Designed by Teresa Dikun
Text set in Old Claude LP Regular
Manufactured in China on acid-free paper

20

Library of Congress Cataloging-in-Publication Data
Soman, David.
Ladybug Girl / by David Soman and Jacky Davis.
p.   cm.
Summary: After her brother tells her she is too little to play with him, Lulu, dressed as Ladybug Girl, makes her own fun.
ISBN 978-0-8037-3195-0
[1. Imagination—Fiction. 2. Play—Fiction. 3. Brothers and sisters—Fiction.] I. Davis, Jacky, date, ill. II. Title.
PZ7.D29117Lad 2008   [E]—dc22   2007008619

"I'm Ladybug Girl!" says Lulu, zipping into the kitchen.

She slips into the chair next to her brother.

"Did you know that
ladybugs
eat
bugs?"

"Yes," he says.

"Everyone knows that."

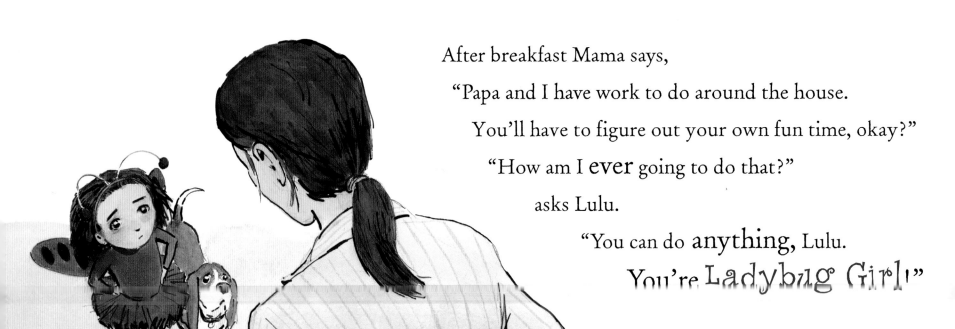

After breakfast Mama says,

"Papa and I have work to do around the house.

You'll have to figure out your own fun time, okay?"

"How am I **ever** going to do that?"

asks Lulu.

"You can do **anything,** Lulu.

You're Ladybug Girl!"

Lulu runs after her brother.

"Where are you going?"

"I'm playing baseball with Sam and Max."

"Can I play too?" she asks.

"No, you're too little," he snorts.

"And bugs don't play baseball."

With a sigh, Lulu wanders through the house.

Bingo follows.

There's **nothing** to **do.**

In the living room there's a wall of books.

Lulu can't read yet, but she knows her letters.

She finds a lot of *L*'s. More than 59, she thinks.

Then she waters her avocado plant.

She takes out her ruler to measure if it's grown.

Some days it just doesn't seem to be getting any bigger.

When Bingo gives Lulu *the look*, it's time to go outside.

In the backyard, the grass smells sweet
and is sparkly with dew.

While Bingo snuffles about,

Lulu discovers a line of ants
marching over a rock.

"Is that rock in your way, ants?
It's much too big for you to move,
isn't it?" she says.

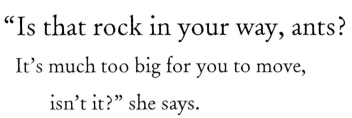

"I can help you! I'm Ladybug Girl!"

Ladybug Girl easily lifts the rock
over her head and tosses it aside.

Nothing can stop the ants now!

"Come on, Bingo!"
she says.
"Ladybug Girl
has things to
do!"

She runs across the yard to the pond.

Her brother calls it a puddle, but she knows it's big—

    so big she can see trees and sky inside the water.

There might even be

a shark

          in the deep part!

Ladybug Girl
jumps
in
anyway!

Her next stop is the old, crumbly stone wall.

It definitely needs her help.

She picks up the fallen rocks and

puts them back on top.

Now the wall is **bigger** and **better**

than before.

It's
the
**perfect
fort.**

Even the toppled-over tree at the back of the yard can't stop her!
Its roots look like angry snakes, but Ladybug Girl
skips all the way down its trunk, not falling even once.

She jumps down and lands with a bow.

"Ta-da!" she says.

Bingo wags his tail.

All of a sudden, Lulu hears the crack of a baseball bat.

She whirls around and sees a ball bouncing toward her.

"Hey!" her brother yells. "Throw it over here!"

She picks up the ball and throws it,

but somehow it lands near her feet.

"Please can I play with you now?"

she asks when her brother runs over.

"No," he says, "I already told you, you're too little!"

He grabs the ball and runs back to his game.

Lulu
glares
after
him.

Lulu lies down, feeling the warm sun on her cheeks.

She knows she isn't too little.

She thinks of the 59 letter *L's* she found, and how she saved the ants.

She wasn't afraid of the shark at all, she built the perfect fort,

and she balanced across the whole tree without falling—

all by herself!

From out of nowhere a gust of wind
swirls the air
with leaves.
She jumps up to chase them.
Ladybug Girl can catch leaves in mid-air!
"Ladybug Girl is definitely
not little!"
she yells into the wind.

Lulu runs up the hill to the apple tree and lifts herself onto a branch.

She can see her brother and his friends playing baseball,

and hears them arguing.

It doesn't really look like that much fun after all.

Not the kind of fun Ladybug Girl has.

She holds her thumb and index finger a bit apart

       and squints through them.

She can fit her brother and all of his friends between those two fingers.

       "I'm not little," she says.

          "You're little."

Lulu sits for a moment
listening to the singing sparrows
and the squawky blue jays.

When she hears Mama calling,

she swings down and says, "Come on, Bingo!

Let's go inside and tell Mama and Papa about our morning!"

Feeling as **big** as the whole outdoors,

Lulu stretches out her arms

and flies down the hill with her wings bobbing behind her.

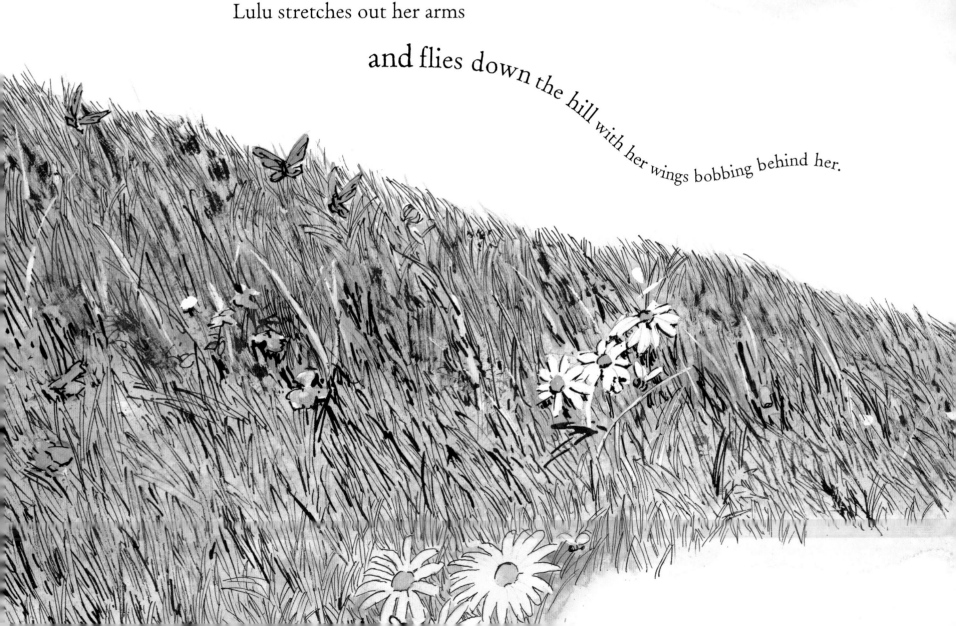